BIRTH OF THE RIVER BAR

MR. BILL

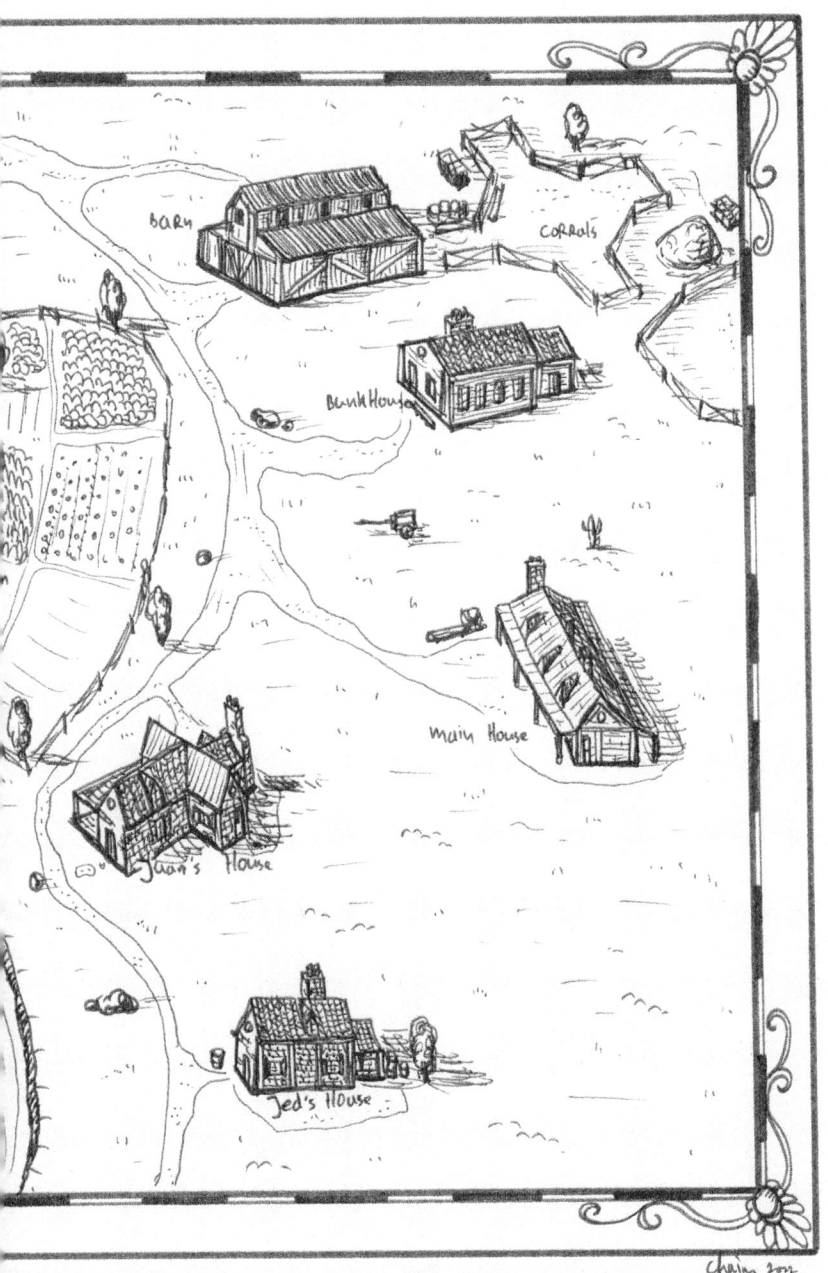

Dear Oncology Staff –
 Thanks for all you
do and continue to do
everyday
 Keep up the good work!
  Mr. Bill

AKA 4-27-42

THE BOY

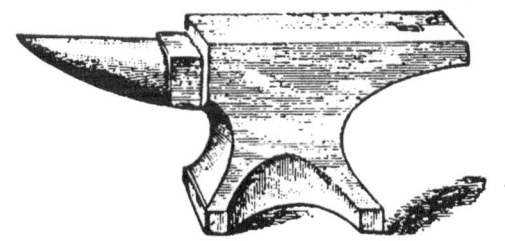

I stood between two giants. Well, they were giants to me since I only came up to their hip pockets. Dad and Grandpa stood looking at the new barn. The neighbors had just left from the barn-raising and my brothers were moving hay and stock into it.

"That'll last a hundred years boy," my grandpa said. "Hand-carved oak beams and good lumber."

"At least a hundred," my dad responded.

I just stared at the size of it. Just that morning it had been just piles of wood and tonight it was a magnificent barn.

"Check on your brothers and see if you can help," Dad said.

I ran to the barn and got started moving cows into the new pens.

Everyone worked on the farm. It was sunrise to sunset, except Sunday which was church-going day.

Cows, hogs, chickens, and crops. It only slowed down a little in winter when we got time to go to school. Come spring it was back to the fields for us.

But it was at school that I met Molly, a skinny little thing a year younger than me, but as smart as a whip in school. I tried to avoid her as much as possible, but she was always being friendly and I didn't want to hurt her feelings. School was okay but I would rather have been in the blacksmith shop with Grandpa.

Grandpa saw my interest in "smithing" and said, "You have a good eye for it, boy."

He took me under his wing and began to teach me all he knew. When I got to my teen years he talked Dad into letting me apprentice about three days a week with the local blacksmith to expand my skills. It was through the smithy that I heard about a railroad job a ways from home. I talked it out with Dad and Grandpa and got their blessing to go try.

"If it don't work out, you skedaddle back home," Dad said.

I told my schoolmates of my plans on my last day of school. Molly walked up to me and I noticed she had filled out some and wasn't so skinny. "We are going to be best friends forever," she said.

I just looked at her and mumbled, "Sure."

I packed a backpack with some extra supplies and started walking east toward the railroad. It took a week of walking and hitching rides to get to the rail head. I saw a line of men in front of a tent that had a sign out front that read "hiring".

I got in line and started asking questions about

Birth of The River Bar

getting hired on. Not too many answers though.

About that time, a short, stout, little Italian guy walked out of the tent and looked up and down the line of men. "Any 'smiths' here?" he asked

I raise my hand just a little so as not to draw too much attention.

"Well, are you or aren't you?" he barked.

"I am," I said. "Name's Frank Sands."

"Come with me then." And he turned and walked away.

I followed him to a low-built building with a blacksmith shop all set up.

"Set up the forge," he said.

I grabbed coal and kerosene and built up a good bed of coals. I worked the bellows to get them glowing hot.

He grabbed two pieces of steel and said, "Align them."

I heated both pieces, laid them on the Anvil, used about a three-pound hammer, and put them straight together.

"Follow me," he said and walked back to the tent.

We went inside and I met the Forman. "He works for me now," said the Italian. Both men just nodded their heads and gave me a roster to sign.

The Italian's name was Toni and he had immigrated to America as a young man and was taught to be a smith. And he was a good one. I couldn't have chosen a better teacher and later friend.

"You can live in the Smith shop," he said. "It will save you some money. You make a dollar a day, unless you work Sunday, and then you get two. We fix whatever needs fixing, we shoe whatever needs shod. If we don't know how to do a job, then we learn," he said.

"See you at sunrise," I said.

"Like hell. We start right now," he grinned.

And so it started. It was like getting paid to go to school to work with Toni. Every animal the railroad used, we had to shoe. Every piece of metal they used had to be repaired. The days were long, but they flew by. On the first Sunday, we had no pressing job so I got to wander the camp and look things over.

I was already familiar with all the crew tents that were lined up along the new lines. They moved every few days as the line expanded. Outside on the edge were the salons and cribs. I decided to give them a wide berth until I figured out what was really going on with them.

The saloons were busy every night since a lot of

Birth of The River Bar

the men built up a powerful thirst through the day. Sunday nights were double busy with the whole crew showing up. This is where the gambling really paid off. Card games and roulette for the big players.

Now, Dad had taught all of us boys about poker. "Just to keep you from getting skinned one day," he'd said. We had learned about tells, double-dealing, and other tricks card sharks used to make money off of the players. I watched the games occasionally, but I would nurse a beer all evening and simply bide my time learning.

As for the cribs—no thanks.

After a few months, I began to really settle in, but Sunday afternoons were awfully slow. This is when I met Big Jim and Pedro. Toni and I were sitting outside the Smith shop when a team pulled up and the biggest man I've ever met in my life stepped down from the wagon.

"Just a shoe," he boomed.

"Railroad horse?" asked Toni.

"Yassuh," he said. "I deliver goods for the Forman all up and down the line. Moving some dynamite today."

Toni and I raised our eyebrows and looked at

each other. "Why not move the wagon over yonder and bring the horse to us?" Toni suggested.

Big Jim just laughed. "You don't like the powder anymore than all the rest." He moved the wagon across a field, unhitched one horse, and led him over to us.

I tied the horse and began to shoe him while Toni and Big Jim got acquainted.

"Do y'all play horseshoes?" Big Jim asked, eyeing our pile of discarded horseshoes.

"Not really," said Toni. "But it sure would while away the time all right."

"I have a friend, Pedro, that might be up to a challenge for you two if you're of a mind."

We finished shoeing the horse and Big Jim hitched him up and drove away. "See you next Sunday if I don't have to drive," Big Jim said.

Toni and I set about getting to iron pegs and four equal horseshoes. Maybe Sunday afternoons wouldn't be so slow after all.

The next week went quickly and came Sunday we heard Big Jim's booming voice as he walked up. "This is Pedro," he said.

A young Mexican man reached out a hand to shake ours and introductions were made all around.

I still remember Big Jim's hand swallowing up mine and I didn't consider myself to have small hands.

"Big Jim, how tall are you?" I asked.

"Foreman says I am 6 foot and 11 inches and I weigh 350 on the company scales."

The three of us just stared at him and laughed.

"I'm just glad I don't have to fight him," said Toni.

Pedro quipped, "That is a sight to see for sure."

We drew straws to sort out teams and Pedro and I were teamed together. The serves were close, but Toni and Jim had obviously played a while more than us.

"Do you boys all like ribs?" asked Jim.

"Oh yeah," we all chimed in.

"Next week we do ribs while we're playing," Big Jim said. "I need ten cents from all of you to get the fixings."

We happily chipped in, if nothing more than to get some variety in our meals.

The next week came and went again and I spent Saturday night watching the poker tables. A lot of money went to very few card sharks. I saw some bad dealing and marked off those guys to never play with.

Mostly, I began to learn "tells". These were little giveaways that players did to "tell" what kind of hand they had. The biggest problem was that too many of them drank too much and were reckless. Others had mannerisms, a phrase, or some other variation to tell if they were bluffing or not. I just mentally put these away for the future.

Come the following Sunday afternoon, Jim and Pedro rode up in the wagon. "Had to make a morning delivery, but we're off for the rest of the day," Jim said. Pedro was his helper, so that meant he was free. Toni and I had finished up all the last of a job that morning, so we were contemplating the afternoon games.

"Where can I find a campfire?" Jim asked.

"Out back, near the horseshoe pits," said Toni.

Jim pulled out a grill, four metal stakes, a small table, and a box of groceries along with some meat.

"Vittles fit for a king today," Big Jim boomed.

Jim and Pedro gathered up rocks for a fire pit and started building a bed of coals. The four pegs were driven into the side of the pit and the grill leveled across the stakes. Jim then began to work his magic. In a big bowl, he started making a sauce, and in a smaller bowl he started making his "rub."

Birth of The River Bar

"Can't tell you all what's in it, family secret," he laughed. We never asked.

Toni and I set up the horseshoe pits and got a game underway. We just played between us while the "cooks" got their ribs started. Jim would build up a nice fire to one side and then push the coals underneath the ribs. He could control the heat to cook the ribs and got some smoke at the same time.

In between cooking and horseshoes, the afternoon went by in a hurry. Jim and I played Toni and Pedro. The game ended up partially even in the win-lose column.

About sundown, Jim said, "Eating time!"

I walked over to the nearby Saloon and bought a big bucket of beer to wash down supper with.

Jim pulled the ribs off the pit and he produced a big kitchen knife to slice them apart. Toni hustled up four cups for the beer and we stood around the table eating ribs and sipping beer.

I knew for a fact we were the happiest four men in the whole railroad camp that night.

After eating we went to the pump to clean up. Jim pulled his shirt off.

"What happened to your back?" I asked.

"White boys down south don't like getting a broken jaw by a black boy," he said.

"Explain that," I said.

"I've always been big, even as a teen. I was walking down the sidewalk and a white boy pushed me off and said, 'no niggers on the sidewalk.' So I busted him one and broke his jaw. That night I got a white cross burned on my lawn. When I went out to see what was going on, I had four guns poked in my ribs and face. They tied me to a tree and whipped me. My mama heard the screams and came out to stop it. 'I recognize your horses and your voices, even with the stupid sheets you're wearing,' she'd said. She must have stunned them cuz they quit," Jim said. "'Next time you see a white man you're dead, boy,' one of them said to me. Then they mounted up and left.

"Ma untied me from the tree. 'I'll kill them, Ma,' I'd said. 'No, you leave the country. They will kill you next time. You have to head off north and west looking for driver jobs. You're good at it and you're big and they'll notice that. Railroad freighter, anyone hiring drivers will be glad to get you. Now let's get you cleaned up and packed. I want you out of here tonight,' she'd said." Jim took a deep breath. "I haven't been back since."

I was mad. That wasn't right. I said as much.

"That's life down south right now," said Big Jim. "And that won't change for a while."

Toni just laughed and said, "The reluctant immigrant, the black man."

Pedro laughed, "I'm the illegal immigrant. Went across the Rio Grande. I'm good at blasting, so the railroad tends to turn their back on that."

Toni laughed again. "Am I the only legal immigrant?"

"No," I said. "My great grandpa came over legal and we have been moving west ever since."

"Well the railroad will help you," said Toni and the others nodded.

"Been on the tracks for three years," said Big Jim.

"Four," said Pedro.

"Ten years," said Toni.

Wow! I really was the greenhorn. "How long will this job last and where do you go from here?" I asked.

They all looked to Toni for the answer. "Doing a lot of spur lines now, but I expect more long lines heading west soon. Most long-line jobs are a year, give or take a few months. We should get eight to ten more months on this line. We hooked ourselves up with a top foreman so the railroad gives him the first shot at each job and we tend to move with him," Toni said.

I had figured on being gone for about a year, so this news was about right to me. I was sending money home each week and Pa was banking it for me. I had been watching the poker games close enough and I thought I figured out a way to supplement that small amount.

On Saturday night, I picked out a table with the fewest card sharks and none of the bad dealers. I watched for "tells" and kept my losses to under a dollar the first night. Each Saturday I returned and my earnings began to increase. I played modestly, sipped a beer, and always left early. Everyone knew the smithies worked early Sunday morning, so it raised no suspicions when I stood and headed out early. People assumed I needed some sleep. Nobody missed five dollars out of the pot either. By the end of the month, I was doubling my wages and learning a bit about the competition and I was content with that.

Sunday afternoons were a regular for the four of

us. Occasionally, some hands came to drop in for horseshoes, but the saloon soon called them away. Jim continued his cooking, pork ribs, beef ribs, pork shoulders or butts, and once a brisket, but we didn't ever do beef ribs again. Those took a long time to cook for sure. How Big Jim rounded up the meat and groceries, we never did find out. He kept his source very secret.

I figured I was sending home ten to fifteen dollars a week. I'm sure Pa was tempted to ask how I did it on a five-dollar-a-week salary but he never did.

I had been at the railroad for about seven months when I got a letter from Pa that suggested I go someplace alone to read it. It seemed Grandpa had died suddenly while sitting in his chair putting his boots on one morning. It was sudden with no suffering. His will had left me some items that Pa would set aside for me. It brought tears, I had to tell you. We had plans for when I returned—now what?

Fortunately, we were very busy for the next week and so I had little time to think of Grandpa and the future. It seemed to take the sting out of the loss and the uncertainty of the future for the time being.

We finally got the official word that the job would end in one month. Toni, Jim, and Pedro were already making plans with the foreman and I had been invited to another small line almost a hundred miles away. "I'll let you know," was the only answer I could muster.

Ma had also written a letter telling me about the wonderful young woman that Molly had turned into. For some reason, I was truly interested in that news and could not think of a reason why.

There was also big news in the camp. A poker tournament on the last week of the job. It would start on Friday and go until at least Sunday. No pot limit, so a lot of money if you could make it to the table.

I quit sending money home and increased my winnings over the next month. I would enter the tournament with almost sixty dollars and the hope I wouldn't lose it all.

On our last Sunday together I told the boys I would return home and maybe join them later if there was work available. I was reeling with a very strong urge to get home, not only for family, but to see Molly too. I still couldn't figure out the draw she had on me.

Birth of The River Bar

The tournament started Friday and used about four tables in the saloon. Tables were set up. Players played until only one was left at each table. Then they set up another table of winners and played them down to a winner. Over the course of the weekend, the number of tables dwindled and the best players all ended up in one saloon by Saturday night.

I was one of the winners. All the time spent learning tells and card sharks and bad dealers had paid off. My pot was considerably more than the sixty dollars I started with, it was now in the thousands.

The players I was up against were good and I had to really up my game, but I lasted to the final winning table that early Sunday morning. Six of us made the final table with a dealer we all trusted as being honest. Each player got to call a game when the time came around. Mostly five card, but occasionally seven card. I noted one player I had never seen before. Western boots, trousers, vest, with a big hat along with a pocket watch and chain. He called himself JB when the introductions were made. He was about as good a player as you could get. I looked in vain for a tell, I then saw him watching me pretty closely too. It didn't take long for three of the table players to be eliminated and I ended up with most of their chips.

I had a big advantage over the other two, and soon one was eliminated when we both read his "tell" that he was bluffing. JB called him and took what chips he had left. The table was now stacked with thousands of dollars in chips. I did not know the exact amount. It was JBs turn to call the card game and he said "seven card." I knew he was hoping to get a lucky draw and pull my stack down some. The game was two down, four up and one down and the deal started. I got two nines, JB did not share anything I could read, but I raised anyway. The next card was up and it was an ace. JB raised modestly. The next card was an ace, and I raised and JB bumped me up just a little. I knew I better pay attention here. Next card was a nine. I had a low full house. I raised. I figured JB had something too. He bumped but modestly, his chip pile was limiting him. The fourth up card was a ten. JB raised me and I called. His chip pile was limiting him but I figured he had a full house.

The last card was down and I got a nine. That gave me four nines. I studied JB's face and he knew

Birth of The River Bar

he had this with a full house, but he wanted to get my chips too. He passed and waited. So I went all in. This trick rattled him because he only had a small stack that would not impact me for another round.

JB let out a long breath and asked, "We still talking table stakes?"

The dealer said, "Yes."

JB pulled out a packet of papers from his vest and said it was the deed for a ranch west of here and it would cover my call to meet his "all-in."

Our dealer handed the packet to the saloon owner who evaluated the property and the validity of the deeds. "They look good to me, but it's up to the other player to accept it."

The packet was handed to me and it included 360 acres of land, a house, a barn, and other outbuildings. It also included some 140-acre parcels of just land. It described a river through the property which meant good bottomland. I studied the packet three times and finally said, "I'll accept his call."

The whole place went silent since this would be the best hand.

JB laid down his aces over tens and smiled.

I laid down four nines and watched a sick look come over JB's face.

JB managed a "congratulations" and slowly stood and shuffled from the saloon.

I sat there stunned. The dealer and saloon keeper started counting the chips. I think there was a small ruckus from the spectators and a few "congratulations" passed around, but I couldn't be sure. I put the packet of deeds in my inner pocket.

"Whatever will you do with your winnings?" asked the saloon keeper.

"Have the bank send it to my hometown bank. I'll give you the address and account number. I wouldn't dare walk around with this amount of cash. Just leave me a hundred to get home on."

The paperwork was done and the banker came down to collect the money. He had two armed guards with him when he picked up all that cash.

I went back to the smithy shop and sat down, still stunned by the success of the railroad job and the poker tournament.

The boys all came in and started back slapping for doing such a good job. Jim fixed us all some more meat and Pedro packed up their wagons and extra horses and started the hundred-mile trip to the next job. Toni gave me my last payday and an open invitation to come back anytime I felt like it from the boss.

Toni would stay around to box up the smithing supplies and then he'd head to the next job. We shook hands and parted ways. I would miss these guys, but I now felt an urge to get home and head west.

I rode the stage most of the way home and only walked a short way between two towns. I rented a room in my hometown and checked the bank to see if my transfer came through okay. I was relieved to find out that it did. And the banker suddenly became my best friend. I then headed home late Friday afternoon.

Needless to say, I was welcomed home by the whole family with a lot of backslapping and hugs. This is when Ma did something strange. Instead of fixing dinner, she just smiled at me and said, "Go see Molly."

"I will tomorrow," I said.

"No, go now," she said.

I was taken aback because this was totally out of character for my mother. So I walked out and mounted the horse and rode the mile to Molly's place.

There were three other horses tied up by the front of Molly's place and three young men were lounging on the porch when I rode up. Suddenly Molly stepped out the front.

Oh my, what a difference a year made, I thought.

She stopped in her tracks and flushed a beautiful pink. "Well, look what the cat dragged in," she said.

It was my turn to flush.

"Frank Sands, I believe, is the name," she said.

"Yes ma'am, and you must be Molly."

She smiled and I melted.

"If I remember right, you like apple pie and a glass of milk." And she disappeared into the house.

I noticed none of the other three men on her porch had any treats. Strange manners for Molly.

She brought out my pie and milk. She then faced the other men lingering on the porch. "You boys might as well leave. Frank and I have a lot of catching up to do."

They slowly walked off and mounted their horses and left toward their own homes.

"Molly, we have more to talk about than you know."

I told her about the ranch I won out west and my plans to go set it up and that I would probably be gone maybe another year or longer.

She just stared at me. "You expect me to wait a whole nother year?" The flush on her face was deeper this time.

"Molly, I haven't even courted you yet," I said.

Molly called into the house, "Mama, Pa! Frank Sands wants to come courting me."

"Tell him to get in line with those other three fellows," Pa yelled from inside.

"My intentions are much more serious, sir," I said.

"Better come out here Pa, I think he's going to get serious," Molly said.

Mama and Pa came out to the porch. "Okay, what's going on here?" Mama asked.

"Well, Frank has a place west of here and thinks he will be gone for another year or more. I don't want to wait that long and he can't court me from that far away."

Pa said, "Do you have something to ask me, Frank?"

MR. BILL

"Well I guess I should ask for her hand in marriage, but it seems awfully fast," I blurted.

"So you want just her hand but not fast?" Pa asked.

"No. I want all of her— just how in the sam-hill does all this work?"

"You asked me if you can ask her, and I say yes, and then you ask her, and wait for an answer," Pa said.

"Okay, I'm asking," I said.

"Yes," Pa said.

I turned to Molly and knelt down. "Is this the right way?" I asked

She smiled. "You're doing just fine, now ask."

"Molly, will you marry me?" I asked.

"Do you remember what I said we'll be best friends forever?"

I know I sure did.

"That was the day I said yes and I still do." She beamed.

I stood up and took her hands and kissed her. Her Ma and Pa congratulated us.

"Ring?" Pa asked.

"Uh—"

Molly's Ma produced a ring and Molly cried.

"When are you planning on heading out west?" Pa asked.

"Monday," I responded.

"Boy, you sure don't waste time, do you?" Pa said.

"We maybe could delay a day or two if needed," I said.

"Well, there is a small issue of a wedding," Mama said.

Molly replied, "Sunday at church. We can get the paperwork tomorrow in town. We'll pack up Monday and then leave Tuesday morning."

We all nodded and agreed that it could work.

"Let's all ride out to the Sands' and fill them in on what's going on," Molly said.

Pa hitched up the Buckboard, and I rode alongside them to our family's farm.

Needless to say, my own Ma was pleased as punch but had a few questions about how we were going to get ready by Tuesday. But the family were all hugging Molly and bad-mouthing me as a potential husband.

When Molly left, I rode the horse back to the stables in town and made a deal with the owner of a Conestoga-style wagon he had sitting in a barn that he was glad to get rid of. He would get me a team of horses by Saturday from a fellow he trusted. He would also grease the hubs and check the wagon out for me. I paid him extra for that.

I picked up Molly the next morning in our family buckboard and we headed to town to get the marriage license, stopped by the parson's to tell him of the Sunday plans, and then I took her to the bank. She was more than a little flustered when she saw the amount we had sitting in the bank.

I then took her to the stables to look at the wagon

"It's really big," she said.

"Not so much when you realize what all we got to take," I said.

About then the livery man showed up with a fine team of six horses. We decided to hitch them up and try them out. They were stout and well-made. I couldn't have been more pleased. The wagon was ready, so I drove it out to Ma's. Molly followed behind in the buckboard.

As we drove up, Molly's mama was on the porch and started to dab her eyes with her apron. "You're barely married and ready to leave already," she said.

Molly misted up a little herself. I suddenly realized the kind of woman I was getting. Short notice and adjusting to married life and pioneer life all in one swoop.

You don't deserve her boy, I thought to myself. *But she chose me anyway.*

We started to figure out what to take. Pots, pans, dishes, some silverware, clothes, and a few furniture items. We had no idea what the farm had so we tried to guess what we would need to get by. We then moved the wagon to my family farm and began packing up there. I took some blacksmith tools, some carpenter tools, a sharp knife my grandpa left me, and a pistol from my Pa. "Just in case," he said.

I built a hideaway box in the wagon and took some cash for the trip. I planned on moving the rest of the cash to a closer bank after we moved.

The wagon seemed to hold all the important things and left room for a small bed in the back.

"Well, we seem to be packed," Molly said.

"Don't seem like a lot compared to a house and barn," I said.

"We'll see when we get to our new place," she said.

I stepped back and put my arm around her

shoulder "Thank you," I said. "Are you as scared as I am?"

"Petrified," she said.

We both laughed. "Let's get you home, you've got a wedding tomorrow," I said.

We drove the buckboard back to her place and I kissed her goodbye.

"See you in church," she said. "I'll be the one in the wedding dress up front."

I didn't sleep much that night, but I got up early and got dressed for church and for the wedding. Fortunately, my old suit still fit, but I filled it out a bit more now.

Molly was a lovely bride to be sure. The three other suitors were looking pretty glum.

I couldn't tell you what the preacher said. All I could do was stare at Molly and wonder what I had done right to deserve her. I must have gotten the "I do's" right because the next thing the preacher said was, "You may kiss the bride."

And so I did.

As we walked out of the church Molly leaned in and said, "I don't feel so scared now."

The reception was a delight. Lots of laughter and well-wishing. People brought different kinds of wedding gifts. Things for the trip. Canned ham, beans, eggs, vegetables, some lace, and crocheted items. Mostly practical items for the journey. We were blessed that day for sure.

We spent our wedding night in the wagon. All I'll say about that is we both were very awkward. We did get some laughs though.

We took the buckboard on Monday and said goodbye to family and friends. It was a hard time for both of us as we approached the wagon that night knowing tomorrow was the day we started our journey. The future was uncertain but exciting.

We left early Tuesday morning without waking anyone at home. We traveled from town to town for the first part of the trip. Then we merged with other travelers when the towns stopped. We usually had fellow travelers most days, but they usually veered off, and another would take their place.

After a few months, the roads were pretty empty, and most nights we were alone. I kept the pistol and a cartridge belt in my clothes, and Molly had the printed packet of deeds in her skirts. We never had any trouble, but Pa said always be prepared just in case. We passed a number of abandoned homesteads, but Molly and I both held our thoughts to ourselves.

As we approached the final trading post before our homestead, "Smitty's Trading Post" we both got tight-lipped and nervous.

"We oughta talk this out," I said.

"What's that?" she asked.

"We've passed a lot of quitters over the last month," I said.

"That's not us, and those aren't our places," she said. But I could sense a little hesitation.

"We have a river on our place and better land, so that is a big setup right there," I said.

"We'll know for sure when we see it," she responded.

"True enough, and it will be great," I said.

We both laughed at each other and sat back and watched the last sunset before we got to the tiny town and "Smitty's Trading Post". It was a strange feeling knowing we were so close to our new home.

THE MAN

We topped the rise and sat staring down at the crossroads and buildings below us.

The last few miles had been a gentle grade and easy on the horses, but we were all glad to have the end of the day's ride so near.

I looked over at Molly. "If your backside feels like mine, I think we've earned a couple of days rest."

She just smiled, rubbed the small of her back, and nodded her head.

The horses could sense the day's walk was almost over and snorted, telling us to get going. As we started down toward the crossroads and buildings, I began to study them. They were just like John "JB" Paxton had described them so I was pretty certain it was Smitty's Trading Post we were looking at.

The crossroads were carved almost perfectly north and south and east to west. The main building was a sprawling affair made of heavy logs and what appeared to be side rooms added on, all made of rough lumber. It sat on the southwest corner, a barn and corrals sat on the northeast corner. Some more corrals were on the northwest and southwest corners too. Horses were in the corral by the barn and some cattle were in the northwest corral. I saw some animals bedded down in the northwest corral which I guessed were sheep or something. East of the trading post was an open field with a couple of wagons and their teams parked in it.

As we got closer, I could see hitching rails on the west and north side of the building. The southside was solid wood with no doors or windows. I pulled up in the lot on the east side and stopped the team near one of the parked wagons.

A man and woman stood nearby and I stepped down from the wagon. "Howdy," I said. "Is it alright to park our rig here?"

The couple just smiled back and the man said, "Feel free. We're the Johnsons."

I smiled and said, "We're the Sands. Good to meet you."

I knew Molly would be visiting to get all the news about the Johnsons, so I set about unhitching, watering, and feeding the horses while Molly set up camp and chatted with Mrs. Johnson.

Mr. Johnson came over and introduced himself as Tom. "Water is over by the trading post. They have a good trough for your horses. They have grain and hay at the horse corral and a smith if you need one. The trading post is open about sunrise and closes when Smitty feels like it. They have about anything you might need out here and the prices are fair."

I thanked him for the information and headed for the water trough with the horses.

As I got closer to the big building I noticed a porch seemed to go around the east, north, and west sides of the Trading Post with doors on all three sides. The south was a solid wall I had noticed earlier. I saw smoke coming out by the barn which I guessed was the smithy working.

There were a few animals in each of the corrals and they were not the quality of livestock I was used to. I went back to the wagon and put feed out for the horses. Molly was just starting dinner, so I had time to talk with Tom.

He and his wife were heading south to homestead a piece of ground about a week away. They had been resting for a few days before heading out. He filled me in on Smitty and his trading post.

Apparently Smitty had come out a number of years before and had a keen eye for business. The crossroads were pretty well-established and he figured the influx of settlers and the number of folks traveling through would need a trading post. He married an Indian woman who was a good cook and he added a kitchen and dining room to the main log structure. She never learned English, but Smitty learned her language. Nobody ever knew what they were talking about and that suited them just fine.

Molly and I finished dinner and cleaned up the camp. The sun was still up when we finished and we decided a walk to the trading post would be good.

We walked over to the east entrance, stepped up on the porch, and entered into a rather large open area. There was a long counter going almost the whole length of the south side of the building. Part of it was a bar and the rest was over a counter to sell all the items on shelves behind it. There were shelves across the other walls with the product separated into categories. The north side had been expanded into the kitchen and eating area. The main room had stacks of bags with beans, sugar, and flour for the most part. There was a small area of tables and chairs by the bar. The lighting was good and the place was surprisingly clean. Two men were having a drink at the bar, a few folks were shopping, and two people were eating in the kitchen.

I took notice of the two men at the bar. They were dressed in buckskins, had beards, and had long hair. They fit the description of mountain men I had heard about. Apparently, judging by their laughing and slapping the bar, they had more than a couple of drinks in them.

As we started to walk by, one of them looked at Molly and said, "Come over here girly, and have a drink with us."

Molly quickly stepped behind me. Without much thought, I grabbed a chair and lifted it over my head. Quicker than I could imagine both of them had pulled out the biggest knives I had ever seen. The look on their faces told me I was in serious trouble.

That is when I heard "The Voice."

"Well now, it looks like two grizzlies are about to chew up a wolf cub." The voice was behind me so I had no idea who it was, but the deep bass voice had some authority to it and the hesitation of the

Birth of The River Bar

grizzlies meant they were not really ready to tangle with him just yet.

"You boys mind if I even out the odds of it?" The Voice asked. The Grizzlies were not about to back down, but you could see their confidence wavering a bit.

About that time, the man behind the counter said, "Would you mind putting the chair down, young fellow? They are hard to come by here."

I mumbled, "sorry" and lowered the chair.

The Voice said, "If you got a knife, this would be a good time to pull it out."

I reached into my pocket and pulled out my clasp knife. I then went into what I thought was a pretty fearsome fighting stance.

The two grizzlies relaxed and started to chuckle. I could even feel Molly starting to giggle.

I looked around and said, "I guess I should have kept the chair."

The Voice said, "Would you put that away? You're embarrassing both of us."

The whole place erupted in laughter. Then the two Grizzlies sheathed their hunting knives and we're bending over the bar and pounded on it. The barman, who I found out was Smitty, was laughing so hard he had tears running down his cheeks. Molly was sitting in the chair with her face in her hands and laughing as hard as anyone.

I turned to face "The Voice". The first thing I noticed was his knife was even bigger than what the grizzlies carried. He just grinned as he sheathed the knife. He was a big man with a graying beard and long hair. He also was dressed in buckskin.

He stuck his hand out and said, "I'm Jed." His grip took me by surprise at the sheer power behind it. "You almost got yourself in a bit of trouble there, young fella. Curb your temper a bit out here. These old boys will fight at the drop of a hat."

"Thanks," I said. "I really did bite off more than I could chew."

"With those two? You have no idea. They are really grizzly bears. Time to mend some fences," he said. "Smitty, does the wife still have stew?"

Smitty said something to his wife from across the room and she answered back. "She still has plenty," Smitty said.

Jed walked up to the Grizzlies instead, "Howdy, I'm Jed. The knife fighter is buying dinner if you boys are hungry."

They looked at each other and nodded.

Birth of The River Bar

"I'm Curly and this is Lance and dinner sounds about right. Especially since this lady can cook."

I reached out and shook hands and felt the same power. "I'm Frank and this is my wife Molly. And we would be humored to have dinner with you."

I thought to myself, "You may be strong boy, but don't tangle with this bunch."

Curly and Lance looked at Molly. "Sorry about the ruckus, ma'am."

Molly smiled and said, "No harm done, and thank you for not chewing up my wolf pup. He is kind of special to me."

All three men chuckled and I knew Molly had won them over.

We headed to the kitchen and scooted some chairs and tables together. Smitty's wife, Swan was her name, brought over bowls of stew, flatbread, and coffee. And folks were right, she could certainly cook.

We sat at the table eating and I started sizing up our three companions. All three were about the same stature and seemed to dress alike. I had no idea of ever tangling with any of them. Jed had a long braid, Curly wore a fox skin with the tail hanging down, and Lance had some kind of flannel hat with three feathers flapping down the back. They all wore buckskins and some kind of moccasin.

"Do you fellows live around here?" I asked

They just grinned and looked at me like, "greenhorn."

Jed spoke first. "I wrangle horses. Catch 'em out wherever I find them. I'll pick out the best and break them. Sell them to whoever is buying."

Curly seemed to be the spokesman for Lance and himself. "We mostly trap, prospect, and trade all over. Usually gone for five or six months and then come down to civilization here for a drink and some provisions. Actually, we've been looking for Jed here to get some fresh horses."

Jed looked at me. "And what about you folks?"

I said we were headed west for about three days or so and that I had a farm out there waiting for me.

The three men stopped about mid-bite and stared at me.

"What farm?" Curly asked.

"It's called the River Bar from what the deed says," I explained. "I plan on farming it."

The three men exchanged glances and I figured there was a lot of information I didn't have.

Birth of The River Bar

"How did you come by this deed?" Jed asked.

"Won it in the biggest poker game you've ever seen. End of the year working on a rail line and everyone was drawing wages and getting a game together. The game got started and the pot got bigger and bigger. A stranger joined in that we didn't know. Must have been passing through or something. Started with cash and ended up calling with his deed. A local branch of the land office verified it was good and put a value on it. I called him and won."

Jed just shook his head. "You beat JB at poker?"

Lance and Curly both shook their heads, agreeing with Jed.

I looked back at Molly with a quizzical look.

Jed looked at me and asked, "What do you know about ranching?"

Curly and Lance started laughing. "He really don't know what he's got," said Curly.

"Son, you just bit off a chunk, believe me," said Lance, speaking for the first time.

"Hey Smitty," called Curly. "You still the land office here?"

"Yep," said Smitty from the bar. "You got a deed to register?"

I pulled the packet out of my jacket with all of our papers and showed him the deed.

Smitty looked it over, noted the notary signature, and said, "It's good."

The three men finished their stew and ordered another cup of coffee. They sat in silence while Molly and I looked back and forth at their faces. Finally, Curly looked at me and said, "You have a ranch, not a farm. It's not a hundred and sixty acres like a farm. It's about fifteen hundred or more acres and lots of open range around it. You're going to need some help for sure."

Jed saw the look on my face and started filling me in. "JB came here a number of years ago to homestead. He figured out real soon it wasn't farming country and switched over to cattle. Bought out a dozen homesteads around him. He was just getting a good start when the raiders hit his place. He was out with a herd and only found the ruins a couple of days later. They killed a wrangler and his wife and kids. They stripped the place and left. They normally don't burn a place because it draws too much attention. That's the only reason the buildings are still standing."

Birth of The River Bar

Questions were reeling inside my head like a waterfall.

"Raiders?" I asked.

Curly took over. "Bunch of no-goods that band together. Usually have a wagon or two to carry stuff off. They ride out to a place and if it looks undefended they come a whooping. The idea is to strip the place and sell or trade it later, especially out in the Indian country where there won't be any questions."

Jed looked up with pain in his eyes. "They hit a place I was working at about ten years ago. Killed the family and stripped it. I found the mess when I got back about three days later."

"I'm sorry," I said.

"So were they when I caught up to them," Jed said.

I looked into his eyes and a cold chill went through me. *Lord, don't ever let me cross this man*, I thought to myself.

"So," Jed said. "When are you guys pulling out?"

"We plan on resting and gathering some provisions and leaving in two days," I said.

"Good," he said. "You go west for about three days until you come to a small river. You turn north and in about a mile it will pass through a log arch with the brand on it. Follow the track along the river until you come to the ranch. It was still in pretty good shape when I came through a couple of months ago. Start settling in and I will be along to get you started in a few days."

I started to protest, but one look in their eyes told me that the decision had already been made.

We ended dinner and Molly and I stood to go. The three said goodnight and went back to the discussion about the horses Curly and Lance needed.

Molly and I walked back to the wagon in silence. My mind was reeling with the evening's events and I was sure Molly was having similar thoughts.

We spent the next day buying provisions which were mostly Molly's decisions. I had the team checked by the Smithy and went over all the tack. I did find a milk cow and Molly and I agreed to buy her. By the second day, we were ready to pull out just before noon.

Jed, Curly, and Lance were standing by the corrals when we went by and waved to us.

Jed walked over and looked up at me. "Did you get the guns I talked to you about?"

Birth of The River Bar

"Smitty had them like you said he would so I got them, but he recommended more ammunition than you did. Said I needed to practice."

Jed smiled. "Smart man, Smitty." Jed waved us goodbye and I headed the team west. We saw the Johnsons heading south not far behind us.

The wagon was heavier and the milk cow was slower so it took us four days to get to the river. I sat and looked at one of the prettiest rivers I could remember seeing. Not the biggest by any means, but clean and cool with trees lining the banks.

A faint track headed north and we began to follow it. Like Jed described, there was a log arch about a mile up. Considerable effort was needed to set the two poles upright and a long log across the top. I also wondered where they got such long logs since the timber I could see was nowhere this big.

Eventually, the tracks split a ways past the gate and we followed the trail along the river. We came around a small bend and the ranch opened up in front of us. I pulled the team up and Molly and I both sat and stared at our new home.

The river ran along the west side and appeared pretty deep. A large pasture was on the west side of the river. On the south end of the home ranch was a stone building with a log roof. North of that was the main house which was stone and log construction. It appeared to be in great condition. Beyond that was a small house which we figured was the bunkhouse. Beyond that were a barn and corrals. All this was laid out south to North on the east side of the river. North of the barn area was another large pasture and then the track continued north.

"Welcome home, Molly," I said.

She smiled and nodded toward home. We spent an hour or so just walking and looking. We started at the south end and walked north, inspecting everything as we went.

The small stone house was solid and well-built. The roof was made of small logs and adobe.

One thing we noticed in each building was they had all been stripped. The stove, furniture, and utensils, all were gone. The cupboards were bare, the raiders seemed to have been pretty good at their job. The house was in good shape, but empty. It was a one-bedroom affair, but there was a start of a foundation like they were adding another room. The main part of the house was open and very spacious. A stove had been at one end and a fireplace at the other. The barn and bunkhouse were solid but rough-built. The corrals would need some work for sure.

We walked back to the house and started unloading the wagon. Fortunately, we had some furniture, and Molly had a bunch of kitchen things.

"I'll use the fireplace until we can get a stove again," she said.

I cleaned out a stall for the cow and turned her into a small paddock. She would have water from the river and I could probably turn her out into the pasture safe enough. The team would be pretty much the same after I cleaned out the rest of the barn. My mind started working on chores…hay… fencing…barn…I got tired thinking about it. Then I grinned and thought, "This is just the start so you better plan on some long days, boy."

Molly and I set up the bedroom and house, had dinner, then sat on the porch listening to the river.

"What are you thinking?" she asked.

I grinned and looked over at her and said, "What in the Sam Hill is Ranching?"

Molly just grinned and said, "I guess we'll have to figure that out."

"Hmmmph, a lot of help you are," I responded.

We worked on the place for two days, emptying

the wagon, setting up a paddock by the barn for the team, and generally trying to evaluate the spread. On the third day, I saw a rider with a bunch of horses coming up the road. It took a while before I recognized Jed.

"Howdy! You lost, mister?"

Jed just grinned. "I'm looking for two fools trying to farm a ranch. Have you seen them by chance?"

Molly just laughed and said, "We just spent two days helping them move in."

Jed's face got serious as he looked down from his horse. "I'm here to ramrod this place, Boss. I think you two bit off a considerable mouthful. No use trying to talk me out of it. I need time off to chase my horses now and then, but I'll be here to guide you most of the time."

I was stunned, to say the least.

"Now I know you own this place outright, so that is good. As to your other finances, you can tell me as we go if you have enough or we need to back off."

He did not know of the chunk of money I had saved and the money I won at the poker game, but I felt I needed to play that close to the vest for a while.

"So, what are you expecting for yourself and where do we start here?" I asked.

"Fifteen a month for me unless I'm off chasing horses. You need a couple of real cowboys to start and then a ranch hand to put up hay, build barns, and general work around here. You have a lot of stock probably running loose east and west of here. Maybe some good horses too since they just turned everything out when they left."

"Well, Ramrod, looks like you just signed on. Where do we find the folks you need?"

"I know of some boys that are getting hungry and a ranch hand that is the best around. Give me a couple of days to run them down. Curly and Lance will be coming this way to trade for some horses in the next few days."

I noted my assent and Molly quipped, "Hey boss, are you going to invite him to dinner?"

Jed gave his approval and said, "I can cook some, but you'll notice not enough to get fat."

He went to go set up his horses in the paddock area and I started to enlarge the corral and rebuild the normal pen. There was a small pasture between the barn and the river which seemed to please the stock enough not to wander.

After dinner, Jed saddled up and rode south again.

I looked over the stone cabin and decided that would be Jed's place. I had no idea what other buildings we would need for the new hands. I guess my ramrod would tell me.

Two days later Curly and Lance showed up and set up some kind of tents by Jed's place. They then began to work with the horses until Jed returned.

On the third day after Jed left, two riders appeared from down south. They had to be cowboys. They rode big and tall horses, wore big hats and real leather chaps. They rode up slowly and took off their hats. "You the boss? Jed sent us."

"That's me," I turned to say with some authority. Molly just laughed and poked me in the ribs.

"Jed said twelve dollars a month and keep."

"Yep," I said.

"Where do we bunk at?"

I pointed to the barn and said, "Over there until we get the bunkhouse set up. It's cleaned up and should do for a while."

"Sounds good," they said and trotted off to the

barn. Molly looked after them and said, "Those are the skinniest cowboys I've ever seen. We need to fatten them up." I just agreed since I had never seen any other cowboys. I came to learn that they truly represented what we came to know as cowboys. Tom and Pete were the real deal and stayed with us for many years.

On the fourth day, I saw Jed coming from the south with two big wagons following him. I walked down toward the stone cabin to greet them. Jed stepped down from the saddle and waited for the wagons to pull up.

"This is Jaun," he said.

A short and heavily-built Mexican man came up to me. "Hello, señor. I am Juan, this is my wife, Luz, and my two boys, Tito and Pedro."

I shook his hand, feeling the power and calluses of a hard-working man. I looked at Jed and nodded. Jed smiled and said, "Juan and his family work six days a week and get twenty dollars a month."

I looked at Luz and the two boys and knew this was a bargain in anyone's books. I smiled and nodded. Everyone relaxed, smiled, and Molly joined in the greetings. I knew she and Luz were going to be close friends for sure.

"So, Ramrod. I have the makings of a ranch. I got land. Cattle somewhere. But where do I start?"

"Did the cowboys show up?" Jed asked.

"Skinniest you ever saw," I said.

"That's normal, boss. Get used to it. I'll have Juan set up below the stone house. We can build his house there, a bunkhouse near the barns, and we'll have to log out corrals for the future. I'll get the cowhands spooking out cattle to see what you have and where."

Curly and Lance joined the group and after introductions were made all around, the cowhands joined us and we started all over again. I stepped back and looked at the group shaking hands and exchanging names. So, this was my ranch and my crew. I was suddenly overwhelmed with the responsibilities.

Juan moved his wagons and started setting up a camp. Luz and Molly moved to the house to start supper. The cowhands set up a target and started roping. Jed, Curly, and Lance went to the houses to finalize their trading. I sat on the porch and tried to formulate a plan to get this ranch up and moving.

Houses, barns, bunkhouse, cattle, finances, corrals, feed, the list seemed only to grow. My stomach only turned a little, but I had a feeling this was just the start.

I saw Molly stop out and talk to Jed, Curly, and Lance as they returned from the corrals.

"How long are you going to be here?" Molly asked.

"Almost ready to pull out, ma'am," said Curly.

"I need you three together for me one more day," she said.

They exchanged glances and said, "Done."

She called me over and said, "Do all you can in the morning. But from dinner and all afternoon, I want you four on the front porch."

We all nodded since it looked to be the only decision we could make.

Luz and Molly had the cowhands set up some big planks and built a table in front of the porch and then called us to supper. I got a closer look at Juan's boys and they were built just like him, only a little shorter. The two cowboys ate as much support as the rest of us all together. I could only wonder why they were so skinny.

` I smiled at Molly and said, "Well the house is good for a while."

She said, "We will eventually need another

bedroom."

I said, "Maybe next year."

She smiled and said, "Try about six months."

I stared, dumbfounded. Jed gave a whoop and slapped me on the back so hard I almost choked. My ears turned bright red and I just stared at Molly. By now, everyone was laughing and congratulating us. I was still tongue-tied.

Jed just grinned and said, "Well Boss, you're going to be a daddy, sounds like." And the laughter started all over again.

Luz and Juan beamed since they already knew what we were in for.

The next morning Jed and I decided on the layout for the ranch. We never knew how important our decisions were that day for the future of the ranch.

We sat down with Juan and began to plan. We left the stone house as the southern outpost and decided to build a house for Luz and Juan between the main house and the stone house. We made plans to move the bunkhouse away from the barn and even found a spot for an outhouse not far from it. Corrals, round pens, and paddocks were moved north and toward the river.

Juan decided where the hay meadows would be, and even set up irrigation from the river. He was a more talented man than I could have imagined. We started to figure out poles, lumber, and hardware for the building. The cost made me choke a little. I wished I had made more in some of those poker hands.

At noon Jed gave orders to the cowboys which would actually keep them busy for days.

Later, when Molly rang the dinner bell, we all trooped to the table. Molly pointed to Jed, Curly, Lance, and me. "You four up onto the porch," she said. Luz went to serve the others lunch.

A table set with four places was set up on the porch. A big pot of stew was placed in the middle with a whole loaf of fresh bread. Four cups of coffee were poured and Molly made the announcement of, "You three have all afternoon to fill in Frank on ranching, the cattle, and the seasons. I expect everything to be covered in detail. Jed can fill in the gaps as we go along."

With that said, she filled up four bowls of stew and cut the loaf into four pieces, and set fresh butter on the table. Turning away, she said, "I'll have more later."

It did not take much encouragement for us to get into that lunch for sure. Jed, Curly, and Lance started slowly, but between bites, they started my education. The size and makeup of the ranch, the seasons of the ranch, and what jobs needed to be done. The list seemed to go on forever but the way they explained it, I knew I was going to remember.

About mid-afternoon, Molly walked out and cleared the table of bowls and empty stew. She then walked out with four plates and a fresh pot of coffee. Luz was right behind her and set down a fresh-baked apple pie. Molly cut it into quarters and served it. Then she produced a bottle of whiskey and put a dollop in each cup. She and Luz then disappeared back into the house.

We all stared at them. Without saying a word, they just recruited one fierce army of grizzlies and one wolf cub.

We talked as we enjoyed the pie and coffee and the lessons just kept coming. This is truly the birth of the ranch.

By the time they were ready to leave supper, I felt my head was going to explode. But I knew what "boss" meant.

THE RANCH

Curly and Lance pulled out the following morning. They headed north having heard from someone who had heard from someone who had heard it on good authority from a second cousin that there was gold and great hunting somewhere up there. Molly gave them a going-away pie just to cement her ties to the grizzlies.

Juan began to look for lumber. He sent his two boys into the hills for logs and posts.

Jed and the two cowhands began to find our "herd" wherever it might be.

"Boss, I think they are probably drifting East since the river is kind of a natural barrier. We will look West first and then head over East."

"Sounds good to me. What do you need?"

"Just grub and horses for now. Will be gone a few days at a time until we figure out where they are. Then we will need some extra hands to round up the herd." Jed looked me up and down. "By the way, Boss, we need to get you fitted with chaps, a hat, ropes, and the rest of the tack."

I stared at him glumly.

Jed only smiled. "Oh lighten up, Boss. It'll be fun."

Birth of The River Bar

His chuckle told me differently.

Jed gave me a list of items I needed and Juan gave me another list. Molly and I hooked up the wagon and made a trip to Smitty's.

When we finally got to the crossroads and to the trading post, Smitty looked at my list and said, "Let's start you an account. It looks like you may be serious about this ranching business."

I grinned and said, "I'm committed it looks like."

Smitty sent me to a Mexican leather shop located by the horse corrals for my tack. This is where I got the chaps, boots, holster, and a wide brimmed hat.

Saddle, hat, guns, and other Ranch stuff I got from Smitty's. Juan needed nails and other hardware so the bill was edging up quickly. Molly just laughed at my new gear, but she did say she liked the new look. I was hesitant about the guns until Smitty said they were absolutely necessary and then told me about the young couple we had just met earlier. The Johnsons. They were ambushed about five days west and were killed by raiders. I did not hesitate after that. We even added a shotgun for Molly since she wanted to hunt grouse and sage hens for some meat options.

MR. BILL

While at Smitty's, I checked up on abandoned homestead deeds with a mind to expand our River Bar Ranch. I also sent a letter home to get funds transferred to a closer bank and a draft for Smitty. Molly and I then headed home with a pretty full wagon, a new look, and armed to the teeth. And yes, I did buy a real knife like Jed carried.

Jed just grinned at me and then said, "Well you got the look, Boss. Now we work on the skills."

Jed started Molly and me with gun practice first. Fortunately, I had purchased extra shells since we were both pretty dismal shots. With Jed as our teacher, we improved quickly, but I knew I would never be a real sharpshooter. But Molly loved her hunting trips with her shotgun.

Now to be a cowboy.

They started me with roping a dummy and we worked up from there. Jed, Tom, and Pete each filled in my eardrums with lessons. Heading, heeling, branding, and a ton of other skills were practiced over and over. I always envied the real cowboys even after my skills got respectable.

I was also humbled when I learned what the title of "Boss" meant. Whenever Molly approached, hats swept off in respect. My word was never ques-

Birth of The River Bar

tioned unless I asked a question. Jed was the reason I accrued some respect.

The amount of respect from every hired hand was humbling to the extreme. I tripped over myself on many occasions, but the hands never belittled or made remarks. I was the boss.

Jed, Tom, and Pete worked west for a few weeks. "Some cattle," Jed just said, "but there has to be more. I say we go east. What you think, Boss?"

I sat on my horse with my three hands and I tried to look thoughtful. "Tom, Pete, you worked this country some, would that be most likely?" I turned to draw them into the conversation. They just looked at each other and then to Jed. He just nodded and they both agreed it was a good idea. I learned a lot about the Boss/Ramrod dynamics from that conversation. In the future, I would not put them into that predicament again.

Jed and the hands packed up a short string of horses and headed east. "Be about a week or so," Jed said.

I watched them slowly ride east until they were out of sight. I took myself back to the ranch and went looking for Juan.

Juan and I had laid out the ranch and he established the timing for all the projects. "We need three more men with all we need to do," he said.

"Do you have some in mind?" I asked.

He sent Pedro off on a horse and three days later he arrived with three men that were more duplicates of Juan. I shook their hands and learned their names were Jesus, Carlo, and Pablo. I hope to get them all straight later on. The bunkhouse was first priority, and then Juan's house, and then the hay fields. Tito and Pedro had been cutting poles by the wagon load and then adobe and stone were turned into some of the finest buildings I had ever seen. Large and very solid, they were a sight for my eyes to behold.

Juan set Pedro and Pablo to building irrigation for the fields. I was a farmer, but this was an eye-opener for me. They would funnel water across the fields.

"We will need to buy haying equipment, boss," said Juan.

"How?" I asked.

"There are many abandoned farms and maybe Smitty can help us," He said.

I sent Juan and his boys off with a wagon and a few horses to look.

Meanwhile, the hayfields responded to the water and the buildings began to go up under the expertise of Jesus, Pablo, and Carlos. The bunkhouse was a long flat roof building with stone sides about halfway up and then finished with adobe walls. The roof was a pole construction with a tile roof. It was something I had never seen before. A porch went all the way around. Inside was room for about twelve men in bunk beds, a table and wash basin, and a few chairs made up the interior.

I didn't know where Jesus found all the stuff, but he just said, "People leave." He would take a wagon and be gone for a few days and come back loaded up. He even found a big table for Molly for the main house. " Someday, we will find chairs or I will build some," he said.

The next house to be built was Juan's and it was the same style of building only bigger with separate rooms. I rode with Jesus to get roof tiles which were made over at Smitty's. I was intrigued by the roofing process and realized the craftsmanship of the maker.

Smitty had a list of local parcels for me to file on and we got the fees and legislative parts done. I was now about twice as big as I started. Smitty appreciated the business, especially some of the guts behind it. He had carried a lot of farmers and lost it all when they folded. I told him who I had working for me and he nodded and said, "You got the best for sure. You are going to need some hands if your boys find those cattle. You want me to put out the word?"

I said to have them contact Jed. Smitty just smiled and said, "That is a surprise for sure. I never figured him to settle down. A long history of loss for that man. Never figured him to find someone like you and Molly."

"I heard one of his stories, I said.

Smitty nodded. "That was a bloody affair and Jed was laid up for a month afterwards. I didn't think he would ever recuperate physically and mentally. He drank hard and fought harder after it for a couple of years, until he discovered his talent with horses. Have you watched him?"

"Just a little."

"That man has that gift with horses like I have never seen," Smitty said.

I filed all of that information in the back of my mind.

Birth of The River Bar

"As you may have heard, Molly is getting ready to have a baby come fall," I said.

"We heard, and Luz is about the best midwife you could have. Like I said, you got the best crew around," Smitty said.

More stuff to store in my mind as I headed back. I had the land plot description with me and Jesus and I went over them on the way home.

"Check them out for anything we might need as soon as you can," I said.

Jesus just smiled and I got the feeling he already had.

Tall green grass greeted us as we drove down the road into the ranch. Pablo and Pedro both came up beaming.

I stood up on the wagon and held my arms out wide. "Magnifico!" I bellowed. I had just made all their hard work worth it, and they smiled even broader.

We passed the stone house and I saw that Jed had started fixing it up and built a little lean-to and paddock for the house.

Juan's house was taking shape nicely and was almost ready for the roof tiles.

Molly was sitting on the porch peeling something for dinner. "I get all tuckered out doing nothing," she said.

"Don't ask me," I said. " I've never been pregnant, but I suspect it's all related."

She threw a squash at me. I grinned and turned toward the barn to talk with Jed.

Jed, Tom, and Pete were all in the barn. "Getting-out branding irons," Jed explained.

Tom and Pete grinned widely

"Let me guess," I said, "You brand cattle with it."

"Boy howdy, Boss," gushed Pete.

"Tons of 'em," added Tom.

Jed just chuckled. "Now you know how important cows are to cowboys."

"Fill me in," I said and I told of my conversation with Smitty.

"Good thinking, Boss," Jed said. "Cause we're going to need more hands."

The nod of his head was like a pat on the back.

Jed lined out the job. "We need about six hands and maybe even Tito and Pedro. We need to get a good remuda right away. We have about eight good horses now, but that is just a start. We found a number of good horses east of here and some are probably the stock that was left. The rest we will have to rough out and the cowhands can finish them." Tom and Pete beamed. I assumed getting bucked all over the country was part of the "fun" too. I just shook my head in disbelief.

Jed and the boys disappeared into the east again along with Tito and Pedro. I saw them ten days later with about thirty head of horses headed for the corrals. Tom, Pete, Tito, and Pedro were in their glory and whooping all the way.

I called Jed to the porch and Molly brought out coffee for us. "Fill me in," I said.

"Boss, you have a lot of cattle up there. Some are branded, but all the ones from after JB left are wild and open to anybody. I haven't seen any sign that some other outfit is close, so I think we are good to get started branding."

"Size of the herd?"

"Hundreds," Jed grinned.

I sat back in my chair absolutely stunned. "What do we do with them all?" I asked.

"We have to find a market or a railhead or someplace to market them. We need to talk it over with Smitty."

As the ranch was taking shape, I thought I could relax a little. *Fat chance!*

I looked down at the corrals and all I could see was Tom and Pete bobbing up and down like corks on a pond of dust. *So the fun has just started,* I thought.

Come dinner time they hobbled up to the house, barely able to move, but chattering like magpies about the great horses they had. I looked at Jed and Molly and shook my head. Jed just laughed.

Slowly over the days, cowboys began to drift in. They all had the "look" and I ended up hiring them. I didn't know his system for choosing, but he got us a good bunch of "bush poppers" he called them.

We had to fix up a lean-to by the barn for a cook shed. About that time, Juan introduced me to Carlos. A thin little man with a Chuck Wagon. Jed approved him right off and I started to get the idea that I had a lot to learn.

The whole outfit headed east one morning and Jed said, "Follow our trail in a few days."

I left Jaun in charge back at the ranch and followed Jed's trail about three days later. My education took a big leap forward.

I was greeted by a rough corral that was already filling up with cattle and a horse corral was set up not too far away. The cowboy bedrolls were tied up

Birth of The River Bar

in a group or somewhere drying out over a bunch of trees.

In the distance, I could see groups of cattle being driven into the corral area. A group of cowboys had lines going as I approached and I saw the branding irons heating up.

"Time to get dirty, boss," Jed said as I rode up.

I watched the scene to figure out where to fit in. Cowboys were roping calves and dragging them to a fire. Two cowboys would then grab them and hold them down. If it was a bull, he got cut, and then another man would brand him. They were then released and the cycle continued all over again. I looked at Jed and he said, "Come with me."

We started by roping calves and dragging them in. I had some experience with heeling, but this really tested me. The boys could tell I was green, but not a laugh or remark was made. Soon Jed had me holding and cutting and then branding. He introduced me to the whole "sha-bang" as he called it

By the time Carlos rang the supper bell, I was a tired man. Carlos brought me a cup of coffee while I was sitting on a stump eating.

"You look good out there, Boss Man. A little more practice with the heeling and you'll be good."

I grinned almost like a cowboy.

My estimation of my crew had just taken a big jump.

Jed grinned. " Come morning you will be stiffer than aboard. Get up and get moving and you'll be okay. Each day will be easier. I have a bedroll for you in the wagon."

I was afraid the coffee would keep me awake—ha!

The next morning I was just like Jed predicted, but I noticed everyone was a little slow and working out the kinks, so I didn't feel like a total greenhorn.

Watching the crew eat, saddle up, and prepare for another grueling day was a revelation to me of the life of the cowboy.

Jed picked out horses and they rode whatever came. Jed gave assignments and they all got started. No complaints, no whining, no balking— just pure hard work.

I looked at Jed and nodded. He smiled back and said, "Real cowboys, Boss."

"Let me try some heeling today," I said.

Birth of The River Bar

He nodded and gave me a horse from the rough string. I had a feeling everyone was watching when I stepped into the saddle. He was a good-looking horse, but he was not the most broke you might say. We did some crow hopping and fidgeting and so I ran him out for a while until he got some of this sass out of him. When I rode back to the corrals, I got a grin from all the hands. I realized I had passed some sort of test and was now accepted at least partway into the circle. Jed just grinned.

We worked from sunup to sundown for a week. I can't remember feeling any better at any time in my life. I finally got to learn heading and heeling when I started on the larger cattle. I still had a lot to learn though.

As we finished up the groups of cattle they were released to drift.

"We will start a round-up in the fall if we find a market. Otherwise, we drift them closer to the ranch and hold them by feeding them a little. These are hearty stock and they have survived really well up here," Jed said.

Is this all open range?" I asked.

"All except what you own, so it is kind of a patchwork. Works in your favor overall," he replied.

I shook my head, trying to figure out just how big our outfit really was. As the branding wound down, Jed suggested I head back to the ranch. He asked to send Jesus up to build a shack for winter.

"We put people up here in winter?" I asked

"Just to keep an eye on things and report if there are problems," Jed said.

What a lonely duty, I thought.

I was pleased to see the progress on the ranch when I finally got to the bluff overlooking it, three days later. Jesus had built a shack close to the cookhouse and started on the new bedroom for the main house. Everything looked neat and tidy from up above. The hay fields were getting tall and we would have to figure out where to store hay pretty soon.

Jed, Curly, and Lance had tried to fill me in on the seasons as much as possible. Apparently, the normal winters were mild here, but more severe if we headed north. The western and eastern ranches could be windy but not a lot of snow. How to get feed, at least to the east ranch, would be something to talk over with Jed.

Molly was sitting on the porch, looking very pregnant. She stood up slowly with her hands on her back. "Well, aren't you a sight? The outdoor life must agree with you," she said.

I didn't realize how sunburned I was until I looked at my arms and hands. "Not much shade out there," I said.

She just laughed. It was good to be home.

The ranch began to get its own daily rhythm. Everybody was up and starting by daylight. Breakfast was finished soon thereafter. Jed's assignments were handed out by Juan and Jed. Soon after, the crew dispersed around the ranch to their various assignments. Jed or Juan or sometimes both would join me for coffee and we would discuss the future work for the ranch. It was a busy time and yet it felt relaxed. I depended on Jed and Juan more than anyone, other than Molly, would even guess.

In the early fall, Curly and Lance came riding in from the northwest. They were all full of stories of adventure and had a hankering to get to Smitty's for a jug. They, of course, had to stop long enough for one of Molly's pies and to catch up on the summer.

"Jed," said Curly. "Do you remember Little Deer?"

"Had a small band about the edge of the mountains up there," Jed said, pointing north and west of the ranch.

"Yep," said Curly. "Do you remember his daughter, Moon?"

"Just slightly. Pretty if I remember right," Jed replied.

Lance chimed in with, "Way beyond pretty now. And, she remembers you. Kept asking if you were still chasing horses up that way."

Jed got a little uncomfortable and colored up a bit. We all looked away like we didn't notice.

Curly and Lance headed for Smitty's the next day. I figured a week of drinking and they would pass back through looking for gold until winter fully set in. I wondered if we could put them up for their winter. I would pass it by Jed.

Jed moved around and didn't say much for the next few days. I didn't push him, figuring he would talk when he was ready.

One morning, Jed just walked up to the porch and said, "We need to talk."

I motioned him up and called Molly, asking if there was still any coffee.

Jed just sat there, stirring his coffee, which he

drank black, until I finally asked, "Jed, what's on your mind?"

"How is married life?" he asked.

Oh dear, I thought. "Jed, I have never been happier, but I have about the best wife around."

"That's exactly what Juan said," Jed replied.

"Are you comfortable around her?" I asked. "Can you fuss at each other without drawing blood? Can you laugh at each other?"

Jed just nodded and looked very thoughtful. Then he spoke slowly, "I met Moon a couple of years back and we crossed trails often while I was chasing horses. I didn't think she could fit into a white community, but a ranch like this has changed my mind some."

Only nodded and waited for him to continue.

Jed cleared his throat. "I need a couple weeks off, Boss."

I nodded. "Tom out Pete can handle things until you get back."

He arose and left. Within an hour, he rode out with a string of ten of his best horses.

We all waited for a couple of weeks with no word from Jed. Curley and Lance rode back through and said they would keep an eye out for him on their way north again.

At the end of three weeks, I saw Jed and another rider on the bluff. They rode slowly toward the front at the south end of the ranch. We all walked out to greet them.

"This is Moon," Jed said. "My wife."

Molly and Luz were the first forward to greet her. Fortunately, she spoke enough English to not be totally overwhelmed.

She was beyond pretty like Lance had said. Raven black hair, high cheekbones, flawless features, and much shorter than Jed. If she did not understand something she would look to Jed for help. That they loved each other went without saying.

Would she fit into the ranch? No doubt whatsoever.

"Sorry about the delay, boss," Jed said with a smile. "Touch longer to find Little Deer than I expected."

"Tom and Pete can handle things just fine. Did you see Curly and Lance?"

"Must have missed them," Jed said.

"Plan a dinner with the crew tonight," Molly said. "We'll eat at the main porch."

Jed nodded and rode off with Moon to get settled in.

As he rode off, I asked, "Where are all your horses?"

"Bride price," he called from over his shoulder.

Molly pushed me in the ribs. "How many horses would you pay for me?"

I grinned at her and said, "How about a wagon full of goods, a ranch, and some poker winnings?"

"You still got a bargain, mister," she laughed.

I did at that, I thought

Dinner was a delight. Tables were set up on the porch and Carlo, Molly, and Luz had outdone themselves. Beef, vegetables, soup, and pies. It was a feast like no other. Of course, Tom and Pete outdid everyone, but Tito and Pedro were a close second to how much they put away.

Jed must have been coaching Moon, she sure handled the dishes and silverware like it was every day fare. Jed beamed and the glances between him and Moon only confirmed what we all thought. He was smitten.

So the rhythm changed just a bit, but the ranch adapted and moved forward.

Molly's time grew closer and she and Luz started making plans. I knew us men would be on the outside for this one. Juan filled me in a little bit about what to expect when the time came.

One evening, Molly stood up while we were sitting on the porch and said, "My water broke— go get Luz."

I went to Luz and she said, "Stay here with Juan for a while."

I looked at Juan and just shrugged my shoulders. He looked at me and just shrugged his.

"Time for a drink," he said and brought a little of some kind of Mexican drink out. It was pretty strong so I just sipped it.

Jed and Moon got word of the activity. Moon went to the house to help Luz and Jed brought over another jug of something stout. "Looks like a 'birthday celebration' over here," Jed said.

I could see where this was heading and suggested we move to the Cookshack. They all agreed and the party moved up to the Cookshack which alerted the hands of the goings on too. They all joined us and Carlos brought out cups to use. There was a lot of snakebite medicine of every type donated to the "celebration".

I was the only one still sipping, but nobody seemed to notice or care.

Someone brought a fiddle and there was a lot of singing too... Maybe singing wasn't the right word, but they thought they were good.

About sunrise, Carlos motioned me toward the house. I looked up and saw Moon waving from the porch. "Might be time for coffee and breakfast," I said, gesturing to the crew dozing and chatting.

"A good plan, but probably not a lot of work gets done today," Carlos grinned.

I shot the rest of my drink back and slapped it on the table of the Cookshack. As I walked up to the house, I was glad to see Moon was smiling. "To the bedroom," and she pointed.

I walked into the bedroom and saw Molly nursing a baby. The tears flowed down and I had to turn away for a minute. I faced Luz and she said, "Juan was the same way." And She smiled.

I sat on the bed with Molly and she said, " I

smell booze. Didn't happen to bring me a pour, did you?"

We both laughed but I said, "Sorry, but no. So… cowboy or cowgirl?"

"A boy this time, we'll maybe change that next time around."

I looked down in wonder. More tears, but I didn't care.

The " birthing celebration" became famous. Not only at the ranch but all the way up to Smitty's. Five more "celebrations" were set in the books before they said enough.

Needless to say, the day after was not very productive, but I didn't care since I spent the day at home enjoying my family and the new addition. Carlos fed everyone, got a little coffee in them, and packed them out the door. Jed and Juan sent them off to bed. Needless to say, everyone seemed to enjoy the " birthing day."

The ranch settled back into its routine and the baby became the center of attention.

Jed finally said, "We need to send the crew east and get ready for fall. I expect we are not shipping this fall so let's get ready for winter."

This meant sending most of the crew up to

drive cattle back toward the east bluffs, establish corrals, finish the small shack, and figure out if we wanted to move hay.

The cowboys, Carlo, Pablo, and Pedro loaded up wagons and headed out.

The ranch became so quiet that I walked around like a lost soul, trying to keep busy.

THE RAID

Things are quiet around the place. All the ranch hands were about three days east up on the flats rounding up the cattle for a fall drive to winter pasture. Juan and his two boys were working on the barn extension at the north end of the main Ranch.

Molly and the baby were napping. I was trying to catch up on my bookkeeping and doing a dismal job of it.

Jed was gone and looking for some new horses to the northwest of the ranch. Moon was not in sight so she was probably in her cabin at the south end of the ranch.

Curly and Lance had come through a couple of months earlier heading north to find who knows what. They were likely trapping, hunting, and panning for gold and they seemed quite content with it.

I looked north and saw Jed riding slowly back by the barns. I saw him stop and speak briefly to Juan and then continued toward me.

"Welcome back," I said cheerily. Then I saw his face, and asked, "What is the problem?"

"We've got some trouble brewing, Boss."

I started to step down from the front porch and

Jed shook his head. I stepped back onto the porch and waited. "We have raiders real close to us. I caught their tracks about ten miles out and they are easing this way. I figure two wagons and about fifteen riders."

My blood ran cold. Raiders were not exactly common in our area, but deadly. They wandered around the far reaches where folks were spread out. They didn't do much scouting or planning, rather they looked for a target of opportunity and attacked. Survivors were sent off to slavery and anything of value was carted off in the wagons. They were merciless and about the most cold-blooded fellows ever heard of. The reputation was too well known by the burned or abandoned ranches and homestead they left behind.

"How long do we have?" I asked.

Jed scratched his beard, shook his head, and said, "Couple hours at most."

"Not enough time to try and get the hands back here," I said, thinking of the thin numbers here at the ranch. " Do you have a plan?"

Jed looked around and said, "I'm hoping that their lack of planning continues. I expect they will come from the west and they are not aware of how deep the river is. If they try to come across we can burn them pretty good. Their next plan will be to flank us. I warned Juan and his boys to get armed and stay out of sight. Moon and I will cover the south end. You and Molly are going to take the brunt of it until they hit the river. We have a chance if they don't do much scouting."

I nodded and headed into the house. Molly was standing at the door and I could tell by her face that she had heard everything. She reached inside and handed me my holster and then headed to the rifle rack. She handed me my rifles and an extra box of shells. I set myself up by the main window and looked up at the bluff overlooking the river. Molly grabbed her rifle and her shotgun and set them up by the kitchen window. She put the baby in the bedroom behind the heaviest wood for protection. Thankfully, he was still napping.

"Any questions?" I asked.

Molly shook her head and peered out the window.

We waited about two hours before I saw a single rider up on the eastern bluff. He was a big man riding a large paint. He had a spyglass and was looking over the ranch. I saw him signal and a

Birth of The River Bar

group of riders came over the bluff and charged the river. Jed had figured it right. They had their guns out and raced right into the river. The depth surprised them and their horses floundered in the deep water.

I brought up the rifle and put a bullet in the first rider's chest. The rider pitched forward off his horse. The other riders were still in the water and perfect targets. I heard Molly start shooting and saw some rider grab his arm and start swimming back. I then started peppering the area with the henry. Two Shots, move to the next one. Unfortunately we hit some horses— but the result was the same. We stopped the charge of the horses from overwhelming us.

Riders were leaving their horses and swimming back to shore. I didn't know how many more were killed or wounded but I knew Jed would say we burned them good. The big man on the hill began to signal for the riders to regroup and by his gestures he was splitting the survivors into two groups to flank us. The two much smaller groups split into north and south groups and moved up to a shallower part of the river. the north end race for the barn for cover. They only made it about halfway when Juan and the boys cut them down. A few survivors raced back to the river while Juan continued to fire on them. The south group followed the river right in front of Jed and Moon. I heard his Sharps boom over and over and then the Henry started a deadly racket. The raiders men ducked, others grabbed wounds, the survivors headed back to the river. I heard Jed's Sharps begin to boom again.

I looked at the bluff and I saw the big man trying to rally his riders when I heard other shots from a distance and the big man clutched his chest and pitched off his horse. A wagon pulled up by him with two men and again I heard a big *boom*. The wagon driver pitched off the seat and the horse bolted with the second man trying to get to the reins. The surviving raiders rode up the bluff followed by the empty horses and the riders they dumped.

All of a sudden, I heard Molly say "You little scoundrel."

I looked up to find a rider running across her garden and turning it up pretty good with his horse. I thought, "You just made a huge mistake," when I heard Molly cut loose with both barrels on her shotgun. The rider pitched off backward and never moved. His horse seemed to get the message and froze in place, seemingly too scared to move.

I called out to Jed and Juan. Juan said they were okay and they headed out to check on the downed riders. Jed had a slight wound to his arm, but he and Moon went out to check on the downed riders too. I saw one man floating face down in the river and Molly and I went to the garden.

Molly never looked at the rider, but she was very concerned about the horse. She sweet-talked her into leaving the garden and actually ended up adopting the mare as her own horse.

We found five dead riders from the raiding party, but we knew there were many more wounded. We looked up at the bluff and saw Curley and Lance staring over at the two riders up there.

"Well, I guess I know who the other shots belong to," I said to Jed.

Curly and Lance brought the other bodies down and three horses they gathered up. All of them had blood on the saddle. We gathered together in front of the house.

"We got lucky," Jed said.

Curly spat a tobacco wad out and said, "If they had scouted at all it would have been ugly for sure."

Jed, Curly, and Lance exchanged a look and all three walked away. I assigned Juan and his boys to bury the bodies. I apologized for the dismal task, but Juan said, "I would rather bury them than ours."

I sat down on the porch and the emotions hit me. I was shaking like a leaf. Molly brought the baby to me and said, "If you're going to shake like that, then jiggle the baby at the same time."

Where and how did I even find a woman like that?

Jed, Curly, and Lance came riding up. They each had a spare horse, two rifles in their sheaths, and their holsters full of cartridges. Jed looked down and said, "Time to finish this, Boss."

I nodded and said, "Give me a few minutes and I will join you."

"No, this is a job for grizzlies and it will be plumb ugly. The ranch will need you here."

"How will you find them?" I asked.

"We hunt them down. All we need is two wagon tracks and fresh graves. We'll find them all right."

I know they would and said, "If you need

Birth of The River Bar

anything, just get word back to me or Smitty at the trading post."

He nodded and they turned and rode off. As they passed his cabin, I saw Moon come out and speak to them. They turned and crossed the river, rode up the bluff, and disappeared from sight.

They returned three weeks later, Jed had a nasty wound across his ribs, Curly had a bullet wound through his lower leg, and Lance had a bullet wound in his upper arm. Molly and Moon got busy with all the medicine skills they could muster. Jed relied on Moon, but Curly and Lance fussed about all the care that Molly gave them, but then again, they never refused it either.

Nobody knows the true story of what happened during those three weeks. Rumors ran rampant for a few years, but only the three grizzlies knew for sure and they never said a word to anyone.

The grizzlies had been laid up for a few weeks, but I could sense them getting restless. So I took Curly and Lance aside for a conference about prospects up north, explaining that I would appreciate their input and would supply horses and grub if they would look the country over for me. They jumped on it like I figured they would.

On the day they left, they stopped at Jed's cabin. I saw him stand between the two men's horses with his hand on each side of the horn and their hands on top of his. I turned away with tears in my eyes, trying to understand what they were bottling up inside themselves.

I watched Jed fidget for a couple more days and finally said, "If you get a line on some horses, now would be a good time to track them down. We could use a few more stock horses and Juan needs some mules and draft horses."

Jed nodded and headed for his cabin. An hour later he and Moon rode out with a small string headed northeast.

When Jed returned a month later, I recognized the Jed I'd known. The horses were really top-of-the-line too.

ACKNOWLEDGMENTS

For my granddaughter, who did the lion's share of the work. I can't thank you enough.

To Dr. Perlewitz and the oncology staff, without which this book would never have been born.

Always to my wife for her encouragement to take this next step in my life.

ABOUT THE AUTHOR

If you see an 80-year-old man driving down the road talking to himself, just ignore him. It is probably me reciting a book. I do not do the Bluetooth or any of the fancy "hands-free" cell phone stuff, so I am not "communicating" so to  speak. When I drive for any distance or sometimes just sit, my mind starts creating stories. This is a rather new phenomenon in my life, and I am trying to adjust to it. I hope you enjoy the stories that come of it. If not, then try to find another soul driving down the road and talking to themselves and see what their stories are.

–Mr. Bill

Copyright © 2022 Bill Mulholland
All rights reserved. No part of this book may be reproduced or used in any manner without the prior written permission of the copyright owner, except for the use of quotations in a book review. All events and characters in this book are fictional. Any similarities to real life people or events are purely coincidental.
To request permissions, contact the author at bethany@bethanyjvotaw.com
Paperback 978-1-958764-03-9
First paperback edition December 2022

Made in the USA
Monee, IL
19 January 2023